MORNING

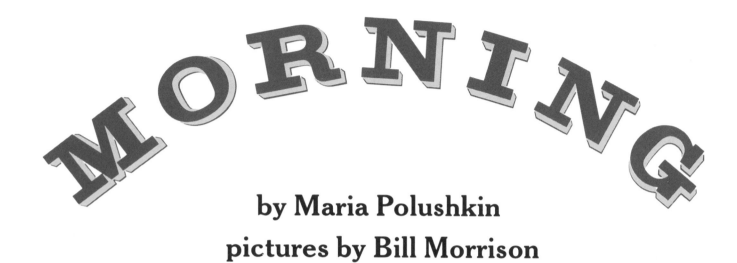

MORNING

by Maria Polushkin

pictures by Bill Morrison

FOUR WINDS PRESS
New York

10 9 8 7 6 5 4 3 2 1

The text of this book is set in 24 pt. Cheltenham Bold.
The illustrations are black halftone drawings with overlays,
prepared by the artist for black, red, and green.

Library of Congress Cataloging in Publication Data
Polushkin, Maria.
Morning.
Summary: After the sun wakes the rooster, and the
rooster in turn wakes other animals, a boy catches
some fish to fry for his parents' breakfast.
[1. Morning—Fiction] I. Morrison, Bill, 1935–   ill.
II. Title.
PZ7.P7695Mn   1983   [E]   82-21076
ISBN 0-590-07871-2

The moon went down and woke the sun.

The sun glowed pink and woke the rooster.

The rooster crowed and woke the cow.

The cow said MOOO and woke the horses.

The horses neighed and woke the lambs.

The lambs cried BAAA and woke the crows.

The crows screamed CAW and woke the squirrels.

The squirrels chattered and woke the cat.

The cat said PRRR and woke the dog.

The dog woke up the sleeping boy.

The boy went out and dug some worms.

KERPLUNK!

He caught some fish and brought them home.

The frying fish smelled very good.

So good, it woke up Mom and Dad.

Good Morning!